# Lunch Bunch

## by Adrian Einspanier

# SAMUEL FRENCH

**FOR PRODUCTION INQUIRIES**

UNITED STATES AND CANADA
info@concordtheatricals.com
1-866-979-0447

UNITED KINGDOM AND EUROPE
licensing@concordtheatricals.co.uk
020-7054-7298

Each title is subject to availability from Concord Theatricals Corp., depending upon country of performance. Please be aware that *LUNCH BUNCH* may not be licensed by Concord Theatricals Corp. in your territory. Professional and amateur producers should contact the nearest Concord Theatricals Corp. office or licensing partner to verify availability.

No one shall make any changes in this title(s) for the purpose of production. No part of this book may be reproduced, stored in a retrieval system, scanned, uploaded, or transmitted in any form, by any means, now known or yet to be invented, including mechanical, electronic, digital, photocopying, recording, videotaping, or otherwise, without the prior written permission of the publisher. No one shall share this title(s), or any part of this title(s), through any social media or file hosting websites.

For all inquiries regarding motion picture, television, online/digital and other media rights, please contact Concord Theatricals Corp.

## MUSIC AND THIRD-PARTY MATERIALS USE NOTE

Licensees are solely responsible for obtaining formal written permission from copyright owners to use copyrighted music and/or other copyrighted third-party materials (e.g. artworks, logos) in the performance of this play and are strongly cautioned to do so. If no such permission is obtained by the licensee, then the licensee must use only original music and materials that the licensee owns and controls. Licensees are solely responsible and liable for clearances of all third-party copyrighted materials, including without limitation music, and shall indemnify the copyright owners of the play(s) and their licensing agent, Concord Theatricals Corp., against any costs, expenses, losses and liabilities arising from the use of such copyrighted third-party materials by licensees. For music, please contact the appropriate music licensing authority in your territory for the rights to any incidental music.

## IMPORTANT BILLING AND CREDIT REQUIREMENTS

If you have obtained performance rights to this title, please refer to your licensing agreement for important billing and credit requirements.

*LUNCH BUNCH* was first produced by Clubbed Thumb as part of Summerworks 2019 at the Wild Project, and premiered on May 17, 2019. The performance was directed by Tara Ahmadinejad, with sets by Jean Kim, costumes by Alice Tavener, lights by Oona Curley, sound by Ben Vigus, and props by Raphael Mishler. The production stage manager was Alex Williamson. The cast was as follows:

| | |
|---|---|
| **TUTTLE** | Keilly McQuail |
| **JACOB** | Ugo Chukwu |
| **HANNAH** | Irene Sofia Lucio |
| **GREG** | Jon Norman Schneider |
| **TAL** | Eliza Bent |
| **MITRA** | Nana Mensah |
| **NICOLE** | Julia Sirna-Frest |
| **DAVID** | Mike Shapiro |

*LUNCH BUNCH* was subsequently produced by Clubbed Thumb and The Play Company, and opened on March 15, 2023. The creative team was the same, and the cast was as follows:

| | |
|---|---|
| **TUTTLE** | Louisa Jacobson |
| **JACOB** | Ugo Chukwu |
| **HANNAH** | Jo Mei |
| **GREG** | Francis Mateo |
| **TAL** | Janice Amaya |
| **MITRA** | Tala Ashe |
| **NICOLE** | Julia Sirna-Frest |
| **DAVID** | David Greenspan |

# CHARACTERS

**TUTTLE**
**JACOB**
**HANNAH**
**GREG**
**TAL**
**MITRA**
**NICOLE**
**???DAVID???**

# SETTING

**A city**

Not unlike New York

**A public defender's office**

Not unlike The Bronx Defenders' Family Defense Practice

**An open office**

Tables, chairs, people. Or just people?
– it's the topography that's important –

**No laptops. Or lunches**

Or maybe just one – *sandwich* – at the end

**Shit office lighting**

The kind that makes you wonder:
*"Can I keep a plant alive in this?"*

**Oh and, just because someone doesn't speak**

Doesn't mean they aren't there
– "listening," "working," "eating," "reading," "banging their head against something," what have you –

# TIME

Dragon Fruit !

Black Beluga Lentils !

Perfectly Soft-Boiled Eggs !

Amidst the distinct fear/feeling that:

*The world is, always has been, always will be (???) going to shit !*

# AUTHOR'S NOTES

**Length:**

roughly an hour (or rather, the length of a "Platonic" lunch break)

**Casting:**

Character's ages, races, gender identities, sexual orientations, physical shapes/sizes/abilities are mostly unspecified and in development we have found various/multiple compelling maps/versions. Names, pronouns, references might change accordingly—or not. As long it's *thoughtful* to the story it's telling. That said, quite practically, this play draws inspiration from a public defender office in the Bronx. There should be more women, trans and nonbinary people than cis men. Racial diversity is a must.

**Formatting:**

A slash / signals an overlap or interruption. Words in parentheses ( ) are not spoken.

For the sake of "reading" this play (as opposed to experiencing it LIVE in "performance"), perhaps CLAP(?)/STOMP(?)—mentally or physically—somewhat violently/viciously upon each centered and isolated asterisk, signifying "a new day." A rude rhythmic reset of sorts.

...

...

...

*(The* **LUNCH BUNCH** *[***LB***] includes* **TUTTLE, JACOB, HANNAH, GREG,** *and* **TAL.***)*

**LB.** MONDAY

**TUTTLE.** VEGGIE ENCHILIDAS AND CLEMENTINE

*

**LB.** TUESDAY

**JACOB.** LENTIL LOAF WITH SWEET POTATOES AND BRUSSELS SPROUTS

    **NICOLE.** That sounds / good

*

**LB.** WEDNESDAY

**HANNAH.** CURRIED QUINOA SALAD WITH SUNFLOWER COATED KALE / CHIPS

    **NICOLE.** Oooouuuu/uuuu

*

**LB.** THURSDAY

**GREG.** BROWN / RICE

**LB.** RICE, BLACK BEANS, STEAMED KALE, SPICED TOFU

**GREG.** How did / you (know?)

**HANNAH.** You always bring / that

| GREG. | TAL. | TUTTLE. |
|---|---|---|
| It has all the food groups | I like it | Healllthy |

JACOB.  Hey—

*

LB.  FRIDAY

TAL.  BBQ JACKFRUIT SANDWICH WITH SIDE
ARUGULA PEAR SALAD

...

...

...

AND A MINT ; )

| LB.  WOOOOOOO | NICOLE.  What's *jackfruit*? |
|---|---|

NICOLE.  —If you guys are ever looking for a / sixth

JACOB.  I don't wanna jinx it /

HANNAH.  Then don't / jinx it

JACOB.  BuT I feel like this was our Best Week YET /

LB (EXCEPT TAL).  YEAAAAAAAH

TAL.  —Hey guys...?!

JACOB.  fuck

| HANNAH.  You jinxed it / | JACOB.  I jinxed it / |
|---|---|

TAL.  I'M GOING TO PARIS!!!!!!!!

| HANNAH.  "Yay" | JACOB.  Shit |
|---|---|

NICOLE.  Paris /

JACOB.  Shut up / Hannah

HANNAH.  *You* jinxed it

TAL.  I know this seems bad, but *Listen:* I'm only gone a
few weeks! /

**HANNAH & JACOB.** "Uh huh" /          **NICOLE.** Paris / ...

**TAL.** ANNNND you know what this means !!!

**HANNAH.**

    We pick up all of your cases / ...???

**TAL.** *Nooo!*

**HANNAH & JACOB.** .../...

**TAL.** It means *Cheeses*!!!

**HANNAH & JACOB.** .../...

**TAL.** Lots and lots of *Cheeses!!!*

**HANNAH & JACOB.** ......

**TAL.** Brie!Camembert!Comté!Morbier?!Tome des (Bauges)—

    *—BAGUETTES?!?!*

**HANNAH & JACOB.** .../...

**TAL.** —Greg???

**HANNAH.** He's /

**HANNAH, TUTTLE, GREG.** "vegan" /

**GREG.** I do love cheeses / ...

**JACOB.** *(To* **GREG.***)* Shut it /

**TAL.** Okay yeah plus you pick up all of my cases

**HANNAH, JACOB, GREG.** ....../

**TAL.** sorry

    **NICOLE.** Not to interrupt, but:

        Did I hear someone looking for a / fifth?

**HANNAH.** shit

    **NICOLE.** Because if someone's leaving, I'm totally down to "Sub In"

...

...

NICOLE.  Is that a / (yeees???)

JACOB.  *(To* **GREG.***)* Who's that/?

NICOLE.  —me? /

JACOB.  No /

GREG.  *(Cough.)* Mitra

**HANNAH, NICOLE, TUTTLE, TAL**.  Who's / (Mitra?)

JACOB.  (Hey you—) MITRA!

MITRA.  What? Huh. Me?

JACOB.  What are you eating? /

NICOLE.  Shit /

**TUTTLE, TAL, GREG**.  (Oh—) heyyyy /

MITRA.  Edamame hummus(?), portobello mushroom(?), tatsoi sprouted grain wrap(?)

NICOLE.  Bit/ch

HANNAH.  Spicy? /

MITRA.  A little /

HANNAH.  Is that a/—

MITRA.  Blood orange, yeah

NICOLE.  (I'm—) Nicole—*I'm free* /

JACOB.  Wanna join our lunch bunch?/

MITRA.  Your—? /

**LB.  LUNCH BUNCH**

NICOLE.  Not / again

HANNAH.  *(Re:* **NICOLE.***)* Is she *??cry/ing??*

> **MITRA**.  I don't know what that / is

**JACOB**.  It's a lunch sharing group. Tuttle's Monday. I'm
Tuesday. Hannah's Wednesday. Greg's Thursday. Tal
WAS Friday /

**TAL**.  *Gruyère/?!?!*

**JACOB**.  Once a week you make slash pack five lunches for
yourself and the rest of the group. The other four days
one of us makes slash packs lunches for you

> **MITRA**.  What kind of—

**LB**.  <u>GOURMET</u>

**JACOB**.  Veggie slash healthy, friendly slash forward. NO /

**LB**.  <u>Peppers /</u>

**HANNAH**.  – Jacob's allergic / –

**JACOB**.  Side or dessert /

**HANNAH**.  – suggested, but not required –

**JACOB**.  And:

**LB**.  <u>No Pretzels /</u>

**HANNAH**.  David /

> **MITRA**.  Who's /

**JACOB**.  We don't talk about /

**LB**.  David /

**HANNAH**.  Or pretzels

**JACOB**.  Let's just say /

**LB**.  David's /

**JACOB**.  no longer in the group /

**LB (EXCEPT GREG)**.  <u>For A Reason /</u>

**JACOB**.  —Greg /

**LB (INCLUDING GREG).** <u>For A Reason /</u>

**HANNAH.** Pretzels Are Not A Side Dish /

**JACOB.** —You in?

    **NICOLE.** If you're not sure, I'm in. Happy to be / *"in"*

      **MITRA.** Yeah sure okay /

**JACOB.** You're Friday

      **MITRA.** Could I actually be / (Wednesday?)

**JACOB.** Friday /

**LB.** <u>HI FRIDAY</u>

**JACOB.** Every morning you'll get a text asking if you want your /

**LB.** <u>Lunch Bunch /</u>

**JACOB.** left in the office or court and telling you what color slash kinda bag it's in.

  —Any questions?

      **MITRA.** I don't / (think so)

**JACOB.** For a minute I thought I was really gonna lose my shit

**HANNAH.** – Jacob takes

**LB (EXCEPT JACOB).** <u>Lunch Bunch</u>

**HANNAH.** really seriously –

**JACOB.** Let's just say you don't wanna know what things were like before /

**LB.** <u>LUNCH BUNCH /</u>

**JACOB.** around here

**LB (EXCEPT JACOB).** <u>………</u>

      **MITRA.** I'm new /

**LB.** Obviously /                    **NICOLE.** me too /

                    **MITRA.** I just passed the bar /

**LB.** CONGRATS /                    **NICOLE.** same /

                    **MITRA.** How long have you been / (working here?)

**HANNAH.** Jacob's about to get his ten year plaque

                    **MITRA.** We get / (ten year plaques?)

**JACOB.** *IF* /

**HANNAH.** You make it

**LB.** – Ten Years – /

**JACOB.** People rarely make it /

**LB.** Three Years

**HANNAH.** Much less /

**JACOB.** Ten

**HANNAH.** Burn out

**LB.** Is Real

**HANNAH.** Shit's

**LB.** Fucking Depressing ...........................................................................
...........................................................................
...........................................................................
...........................................................................
...........................................................................
...........................................................................

**JACOB.** Well okay then. Crisis averted /

**HANNAH.** Don't / (jinx it)

**JACOB.** —Where were we?

**TUTTLE.** —Hey guys...?!

**JACOB.** FucK

**HANNAH**. *I Said* / Don't—

**JACOB**. I jinxed it

**TUTTLE**. ...I'm doing Whole 30!!! ...

**JACOB**. —*Whole/???*

**HANNAH & TUTTLE**. 30 /

**HANNAH, GREG, TUTTLE**. No sugar. No grains. No dairy. No beans. No MSG. No alcohol. No fun. Basically: organic meats and veggies /

**TUTTLE**. And I'm a vegetarian so that means: /

**HANNAH, GREG, TUTTLE**. VEGGIES

| **JACOB**. | **TAL**. |
|---|---|
| You gotta be fucking kidding me | No *Cheese?* |

**TUTTLE**. It's just 30 days. After that I can start reincorporating things back into my diet, one at a time, slowly, methodically, to isolate the culprits

**JACOB**. The—

**TUTTLE**. Whatever's been giving me occasional gas and near constant feelings of worthlessness

**HANNAH**. Did someone just / (fart?)

 **NICOLE**. Sorry

**JACOB**. You're in

    ...

    ...

 **NICOLE**. What? Who? Me? SER/IOUSLY!

**JACOB**. Go on Prime. Buy a cookbook and a cast-iron. Don't. Make me regret this

 **NICOLE**. What's a cast iron? —WAIT. NO DON'T TELL ME HAHAHAHA KIDDING – I'll google it – THANKYOUTHANKYOUTHANKYOU /

**JACOB**.  You're Monday

**LB**.  <u>HI MONDAY</u>

    **NICOLE**.  You won't regret this

**JACOB**.  I'm going to regret this

**HANNAH**.  Yeah. Probably

    **TAL**.  ...*Paris* !

...

*

(The LUNCH BUNCH now includes NICOLE,<br>MITRA, JACOB, HANNAH, and GREG.)

**LB**.  <u>MONDAY</u>

**NICOLE**.  <u>MIXED NUT BUTTER AND JELLY ON<br>/ LEFTOVER PITA BREAD ?</u>

**HANNAH**.  <u>MOLDY PITA BREAD ?!</u>

**NICOLE**.                                                    – wait, really, it's not that –

                                                       so/rry

**JACOB**.  I already regret this

**HANNAH**.  Totally

**NICOLE**.                                                    it won't happen again /

*

**LB**.  <u>TUESDAY</u>

**JACOB**.  LEMON TAHINI GODDESS NOODLES WITH<br>TEMPEH "BACON" AND GARLIC BROCCOLINI

...

...

...

**GREG.**  Jacob

**HANNAH.**         this

**MITRA.**             is

**NICOLE.**                 SoGood

        …

        …

        …

**JACOB.**              I'll send you the recipe

        *

**LB.**  FRIDAY

**MITRA.**  COZY TURMERIC BLACK-EYED PEA STEW
WITH CRUSTY WHOLE GRAIN BREAD

        …

        …

**MITRA.**  I left yours in the

**JACOB.**  —got it

**TUTTLE.**  Looks good ; )

      —I love turmeric

**JACOB.**

    Is this…*Adobo?/?*

**MITRA.**  yeah

**JACOB.**  nice touch /

**MITRA.**  thanks

        …

**MITRA.**  *(On the phone.)* Hi yes this is—

—I'm your new

Uh huh, Uh huh, Uh huh

—Yeah no I can see why you

—Sorry would you mind

—No it's just     You're     You're speaking a little (?uh?)

—Hello?

—*He(llo)*

...

She hung up on me

**TUTTLE.**

—Ms. Tucker?

**MITRA.** yeah /

**TUTTLE.** She does that

**MITRA.**

—should I call her back?

**TUTTLE.**

...in a minute...

                                    ...

**TUTTLE.** shit

...

(*Re: her shoes.*) —Do these match?

                          ...

**HANNAH.** —Has anyone seen Greg?

**MITRA.** I think he's on intake

**HANNAH.** got it /

**TUTTLE.**  Oof —Again?

**MITRA.**  ?/?

**TUTTLE.**  Last week he got *Six New Cases* in one day

**MITRA.**  —Is that *?a / lot?*

**TUTTLE.**  Two weeks ago I got *Four* then had a long cry in the coat closet

**MITRA.**  —Which (closet is that?)

**TUTTLE.**  Around the corner. First door on the left —The coats absorb the sounds of sobbing in the winter —You should try it

**MITRA.**  ...

thanks

**TUTTLE.**  Poor Greg. I don't think he's won a hearing in months/...

**HANNAH.**  He just got overnights for the González family

**TUTTLE.**  —ACS agreed to that??? —What Judge?

**HANNAH.**  Tompkins

**TUTTLE.**  *I loooove Tompkins...* —OU! I just remembered!

**HANNAH & MITRA.**  ...

**TUTTLE.**  I had another dream I          killed Judge White

**MITRA.**  —wh/at?

**HANNAH.**  —Method?

**TUTTLE.**

Slow...            Asphyxiation... —Do you think / that's bad?

**HANNAH.**  That's not a nightmare. That's my fucking fantasy

**TUTTLE.**

—I could have sworn something bad happened... —You sure there wasn't an issue with the shelter?

**HANNAH.** You're thinking of the Richards

**TUTTLE.** Am I/?

**HANNAH.** They got fucked because of their history with DV /

**TUTTLE.** —ugh *that?* That whole thing was / *bOgus*

**HANNAH.** She's at single women's, he's with the brother, kids are out of foster staying with an aunt in North Carolina /

**TUTTLE.** *North Caro/lina?!*

**HANNAH.** keep up

**TUTTLE.** ; (

Greg's resilient... He never cries in the coat closet

—No, Wait, ONCE!

**HANNAH.** That was because his mom had cancer

**TUTTLE.** HIS MOM HAD CANCER ?!?!

**HANNAH.** *? yeahhh / ?*

**TUTTLE.** —IS SHE *??? O/KAYYY ???*

**HANNAH.** How the fuck would I know

...

**TUTTLE.** One time Hannah got *FIVE NEW CASES* on intake, but then she won two 1028s the same day

**MITRA.** —*Seriously???*

**HANNAH.** "1028 *Kween*"                    —You're not a cog. You're a wrench /

**TUTTLE.**                              **HANNAH.**
"Fucking up the machine"        Fucking up the machine

**HANNAH.** I grabbed Greg's. Bringing it to court. Later

...

**TUTTLE**.  I'm a wrench, I'm a wrench, I'm a wretch

...*oughhh/*...

**MITRA**.  How does she do it?

**TUTTLE**.

I don't know. Some of the cases, I look at them and think "This is bad. This is *really* bad," and she's just like "Oh? This?"

—You should follow her. She's good

**NICOLE**.  (So this is—) Tooooom-rick?

**MITRA**.  ...

yeah

**TUTTLE**.  (It's—) anti-inflammatory. Have you tried—

**MITRA**.  activating it with pepper

**TUTTLE**.  You're good ; )

 **HANNAH**.  —Forgot my badge

**MITRA**.  ...

Hey—

 **HANNAH**.  ???

**MITRA**.  ...

nothing

 **HANNAH**.  ...

  All right. I'm out

   ...

   ...

**MITRA**.  Not to be— But does she...*Have something?*

– on *Her Eye?* –

Lid

**TUTTLE.** Oh, yeah, she gets those

I can never remember what they're called… Something French…?

**MITRA.** ?/?

**TUTTLE.** sounding…? A swollen gland I think. They usually last somewhere between ten days and two years

**MITRA.** *fuuuuuck*

**TUTTLE.** Last year she had this one that was *HUUUUGE.* She had to get it surgically removed because of like "blocked vision" or something

**MITRA.** that sucks

**TUTTLE.** —are you kidding???

**MITRA.** To have something that *?Big?* – on your face

**TUTTLE.** That sounds *AMAZING*

**MITRA.** ?/?

**TUTTLE.** An outer manifestation of "All This"

I wish it was contagious…

**MITRA.** …/

**TUTTLE.** All right. I'm out too. Home visit. *Eaughk!* Enjoy *; )*

…

**NICOLE.** I think Jacob hates me

**MITRA.** I don't think he /

**NICOLE.** Shit —Did I say that out loud? I'm trying to be more confident and less annoying /

*

**LB.** <u>MONDAY</u>

**NICOLE.** I JUST THREW A LOT OF THINGS I LIKE TOGETHER. I'M NOT QUITE SURE WHAT TO CALL IT!

...

...

**HANNAH.**  Witness prep

**MITRA.**  Supervision

**NICOLE.**

    I'll just (...)

...

**JACOB.**  What the fuck is this?

**GREG.**

    I think it's...*Tomatoes?*

**JACOB.**  —Is everyone's A game too much to ask /

**GREG.**  "Everyone's A game is different" /

**JACOB.**  I'm not asking for A Michelin Star. I'm asking for
a four and a half star yelp review

**GREG.**

    (Want some—) hot sauce?

**JACOB.**

    How can you (eat that?)

    I can't even say it

**GREG.**  It's just food

**JACOB.**  *"Just"*

    "Food"

**GREG.**

    ...?

**JACOB.**  What Do You Eat—*at home*

**GREG.**

the basics?

**JACO.** *...Define...*

..."Basics"...

**GREG.**

Grains(?), Legumes(?), A Vegetable or Two(?)

**JACOB.**

...Keep going...

**GREG.** ...? I like...? tahini

**JACOB.**

—Do You: *Go "Out"*

**GREG.** To...par/ties?

**JACOB.** *To. Eat*

**GREG.** ......

**JACOB.** You've gotta be fucking kidding me

**GREG.** I'm noticing a theme(?), a thread(?), something or other around which we seem to be circling (...)

**JACOB.** ding-ding-ding

**GREG.**

**JACOB.** How do I say this? I have low "expectations," little "faith," when it comes to the law, government, organized religion, things that fall under the umbrella of "humanity" and its "systems." And *soooo*, I seek my jollies, my *joy,* my "bliss," what have you – some semblance of *control* – in this one area, this one *"Arena,"* of my existence

**GREG.**

*Joy* is a vulnerable emotion

**JACOB.**  I can handle it

**GREG.**

*—Can you??*

**JACOB.**

****Definitely****

**GREG.**

I was listening to this podcast – the other morning – on my way to work

**JACOB.**  .../

**GREG.**  *When I look at my child, sound asleep, in their bed, I'm filled with *Joy* at the recognition of my love for them. And then, almost immediately, from that *Joy* stems deep panic and paralyzing dread as I imagine all the ways this child – and my *Joy* – might be taken from me*

**JACOB.**

—You have: *"A Child?"*

**GREG.**  No

It's an example. From the host—of the podcast

**JACOB.**  ...

ACS

**GREG.**  —what ("did they do") this time?

**JACOB.**  An example—of how that child might be taken from you

...

**MITRA.**  *(On the phone.)* Hi yes this is—

Your (new)—

*—I'm-just-calling-you-back-about*

...

shit

...

JACOB.  What is that? What are you—

GREG.  (It's—) a book

JACOB.  ......

GREG.  It's called: *Flow?*

JACOB.  —Is it about *"Yoga"*

GREG.  It's hard to describe...

JACOB.  .../

GREG.  It sounds kind of...

JACOB.  .../

GREG.  douche-y...

JACOB.  ...

GREG.  I haven't finished it yet. But so far—from what I can gather

JACOB.

GREG.  It's about happiness, anxiety, boredom, chronic dissatisfaction, escalating expectations, fixation on achievement, our ultimate aloneness —Basically, existential dread     —Really it's about the fact that there's no way our "affluent" "scientific" supposedly "sophisticated" world is going to provide us with happiness, and that no matter how much energy we devote to its care the body will give out

—Eventually—

**JACOB.** ...

*Why Are You Vegan* /

**GREG.** I'm flexible. I eat cheese —And quiche, occasionally /

**JACOB.** This is inedible /

**GREG.** Do you think it's possible that with this "Lunch Bunch," you're giving up on the world and cultivating your own "Little Garden"—so to say

**JACOB.**

My own…*"Little Garden"* /

**GREG.** – metaphorically speaking / –

**JACOB.** I'M A PUBLIC FUCKING DEFENDER

**GREG.**

I think it's important to remember that "seeking pleasure" is a reflex response built into our genes for the preservation of the species

**JACOB.**

**GREG.** The pleasure we take in eating exists as an evolutionary tool meant to ensure that the body will get the nourishment it needs—to survive. Not for the purpose of our own…"Personal"…Advantage /

**JACOB.** …Where are you going / with this?

**GREG.** Pain and pleasure occur in consciousness. As long as we obey these socially conditioned stimulus response patterns that exploit our biological urges we are controlled – *From The Outside.* How might we learn to channel our thoughts and desire*s – From Within*

**JACOB.**

—What are you like: Christian? Budd/hist?

**GREG.** Control over consciousness cannot be institutionalized

**JACOB.**

Do you know how long it's been since I've had some good news around here?

Do you know how long it's been since I've returned a kid to one of their mother fucking parents?

**GREG.**  —You got unsupervised visits for the Sánchez / kid

**JACOB.**  I need A WIN. I need *A Win* – ORRRR !!

*ORRRR !!!,* I need a TWELVE TO FOURTEEN HOUR VEGGIE RAMEN WITH A PERFECTLY SOFT-BOILED EGG

...

I'm not eating this

...

"oops"

...

**GREG.**  I would have taken that

**JACOB.**

You can find me – At the halal stand

...

...

...

**NICOLE.**  I think they're talking about me

**MITRA.**  —Who?

**NICOLE.**  Greg. And Jacob

**MITRA.**  I think they're talking about a book? Something sort of...*Douche-y?*

**NICOLE.**  When Tal comes back – From Paris – I'm through

**MITRA.** ...

...

**NICOLE.** *(Re: her Lunch Bunch.)* What do you / (think?)

**MITRA.** Creative

**NICOLE.** ...In a / (good way?)

**MITRA.** sorry       —Mouth's full

    **TUTTLE.** Hey, what'd y'all do this weekend?

**MITRA.** Netflix             **NICOLE.** Hulu

**TUTTLE.** That's F/un!

**MITRA.** —you? /

**TUTTLE.** Work Sat, Bed Sun, Took a bunch of pics of my cat —Wanna see?

**MITRA & NICOLE.** Sure

...

**MITRA.** What's its name?

**TUTTLE.** Harper

**MITRA.** Awwh             **NICOLE.** Cuuute

**TUTTLE.**

    (She's a—) photo slut

      **GREG.** (Y'all talking about—) Harper?

**TUTTLE.** yeah

...

**GREG.** —lookin gooooood

**NICOLE.** Hey Greg, what do you / (think?)

**GREG.** —Creative

**HANNAH**. WHAT THE FUCK IS THIS

...

    oh

    Nicole...

    hey

**NICOLE**.  I just, um?, put a lot of things, I like? ...together? I wanted to practice baking. And uh, blanching

**HANNAH**.

    —In that order?

**NICOLE**.

    *yes...?*

**HANNAH**.

    Jacob's gonna be pissed /

**GREG**.  I think he liked it /

**HANNAH**.  Word of advice: Monday's a really important day. It sets the tone for the rest of the week

**NICOLE**.

    I'll find a recipe

**HANNAH**.  It's the twenty-first century. With a few clicks on the internet and a trip to Trader Joe's you can replicate the feasts of past emperors...In under thirty minutes /

**NICOLE**.  Got it /

**HANNAH**.  I'm grabbing Jamaica cart —Anyone want anything?

**GREG**.  No thanks...          **MITRA**.  We're good...

**HANNAH.** *David...*

<u>**TUTTLE & GREG.** pretzels...</u>

<u>**NICOLE & MITRA.** —what ?</u>

**HANNAH.** —nothing

...

...

**NICOLE.** I'll be right (back)

...

**MITRA.** Coat—?

**GREG.** Yep

**MITRA.** closet...

...

**MITRA.** Should we—?

**GREG.** – in a minute –

...

...

**MITRA.** *(Re: Nicole's Lunch Bunch.)* This is *reallllly b/ad*

**GREG.** yeahhh...

...

**MITRA.** Did Hannah's, uh? *French thing?* switch eyes?

**GREG.**

Oh. Huh

I guess it did

**MITRA.**

Is that / (normal?)

HANNAH.  (Forgot my) —wallet

<u>**MITRA & GREG.**</u>  ...

HANNAH.  What are you /

*

<u>**LB.**  WEDNESDAY</u>

HANNAH.  SPICY PEANUT SOBA NOODLES TOPPED
WITH SHAVED CARROT AND CUCUMBER SALAD

...

HANNAH.  —Like it?

GREG.  yeah

HANNAH.  —Like it?

NICOLE.  OHMYGODmmmmm!/

HANNAH.  (It's a—) new recipe /

JACOB.  I'd prefer if it didn't come with a side of back-
patting

MITRA.  It's great Hannah

HANNAH.  The noodles are one hundred percent buckwheat
and I subbed tamari

—gluten free

JACOB.  If you toast the seeds next time it'll bring out the
nuttiness

HANNAH.

I did

JACOB.  —what?

HANNAH.  *toast them*

JACOB.  ...

HANNAH.  ...

**JACOB.**  —conference. I'm out

...

**MITRA.**  —citrus or vine/gar?

**HANNAH.**  citrus

—order to show cause. Later

...

...

**MITRA.**  Is Jacob always /...

**TUTTLE.**  Like that? – Basically

**MITRA.**

—Why doesn't she/...?

**TUTTLE.**  Deck him?

His desserts are *Really* good

—Has he made his coconut carob chip cookies?

**MITRA.**  not yet

**TUTTLE.**            get ready

...

**TUTTLE.**  So how are ya? You "adjusting?" (Have you had your—) First week in court? Intake coming up?

**MITRA.**  Yeahhh. It's a bit...*Overwhelming?*

**TUTTLE.**  The work or—/?

**MITRA.**  everything

**TUTTLE.**  ah yes, *"Everything"* ...My favorite...

**MITRA.**  ...

The summer after my 2L, I interned at one of those big corporate firms

(I was—) Trying to make a dent in my loans /

**TUTTLE.**  I should do / that...

**MITRA.**  I was doing litigation

**TUTTLE.**  Oh woo/oow

**MITRA.**  *Which* – at the time – sounded cool. But really it was just hours and hours of document review

**TUTTLE.**

So that's what they do...In those big corporate towers

**MITRA.**  – Basically –

—That and eat lunch /

**TUTTLE.**  ?I think my stomach just growled?/

**MITRA.**  They take The Whole Hour

**TUTTLE.**  *!!!!*

I've always wanted:                    *Une Heure*

**MITRA.**

When I was there, we could expense up to eighty-five dollars a day [**TUTTLE.**  holy shit!!!] and if I worked over ten hours [**TUTTLE.**  Who doesn't work over ten hours???] I could bill the client for dinner. At eight fifteen, there was a line of black cars wrapped around the building. "Free ride if ya work past eight"

**TUTTLE.**

So dreamy. So douche-y

**MITRA.**  yeahhh...

**TUTTLE.**  —Do you miss it?

**MITRA.**

no

I wanted to do something that *"Mattered"* /

**TUTTLE.**  I remember that feeling /

**MITRA.**  And I've always liked an underdog

**TUTTLE.**

   I thought you were gonna say "Undercut"

**MITRA.**

   that too

**TUTTLE.**

   —How long does it take you to get home?

**MITRA.**  An hour. Give or take. You?

**TUTTLE.**  Hour thirty – Give. I might move

                         ...

**TUTTLE.**  ...cheese...

**MITRA.**  —what?

**TUTTLE.**  nothing

                         ...

**MITRA.**  —How do you do it?

**TUTTLE.**  *?Doooo?* /

**MITRA.**  Whole 30. It seems...impossible

**TUTTLE.**  The background on my phone says "Sugar is
   poison" "Dairy is poison"

**MITRA.**  ???

**TUTTLE.**  – to remind me –

**MITRA.**  That sounds...*Bleak*

**TUTTLE.**  Oh. No. It's cheerful. I wrote it in pink

                         ...

**TUTTLE.**  —See?

...

**MITRA.**  —Nice font

**TUTTLE.**

thank you ; )

...

**TUTTLE.**  Lunch Bunch was pretty healthy to begin with though, and in general I try to be pretty careful about what I put into my body—except for when I'm dating, or you know, "dating"

I like having something to fixate on. Something to google for forty-five minutes before bed. "Vegetarian Whole 30 Recipes" "Could my apathy be a result of a food allergy" "How to acquire *French Things*." Something to help me forget about global inequality, environmental doom, Judge White in general. Something to drown out the sounds of children screaming for their parents and their parents screaming back for them —I have a lot of night terrors

I really want "A Hobby," but I suck at sports —! I've been getting into skin care! "Natural products." Anti-aging. I'm on the prowl for a really good mineral sunscreen/...

**MITRA.**  ?/?

**TUTTLE.**  SPF will kill you – "Chemicals" or something. That said, I'll probably just end up buying whatever they sell at Trader Joe's. I like their packaging —It's affordable, and their employees always seem really happy. Sometimes I wonder: If we sold groceries would people wanna shop here? If I was a cashier would anyone wanna check out with me? —Do you ever think about that?

**MITRA.**

Not in those terms – Specifically. But I have a metaphor
for life that involves dumplings

**TUTTLE.**


oh wow /

**MITRA.**  —what?

**TUTTLE.**

I love dumplings

**MITRA.**


dumplings are good

**TUTTLE.**


yeah…

                                        …

**MITRA.**  —Is that true?

**TUTTLE.**  (—What?)

**MITRA.**  about sugar and dairy

**TUTTLE.**

A lot of things are poison

**MITRA.**  Like…/

**TUTTLE.**  Self-righteousness, social media, not asking
questions, most people I "date"

—but yeah they're basically poison

!Also! chemical run-off from Big Sugar is ruining the Everglades

—I have a friend – in Miami – I can send you a link

**MITRA.**

thanks. I'm trying to eat less…

*—sugar*

...

**TUTTLE.**  I'm having that feeling you get when you have an email waiting. I can't tell if it's bad or good… Maybe it's boring? I can feel my heart beating. BaBum BaBum BaBoom. Inside my chest

—Do you ever feel like there's no time?

**GREG.**  There's time, I think we just waste most of it /

**TUTTLE.**  GEEZUS Greg! You scared the shit out of me

**GREG.**  —sorry. (Was just—) "reading"

**TUTTLE.**

I'm gonna check my email now

.../

*

**LB.**  FRIDAY

**MITRA.**       ROASTED VEGGIE TACOS WITH CHIMICHURRI SIDE FIESTA CORN SALAD

...

**NICOLE.** Hey guys, I found this recipe that I'm really excited about and a pay-what-you-can cooking class for over the weekend! —Mitra! ohmygod! this is delicious!!!

**MITRA.** thanks Nicole. Looking forward to...

**NICOLE.** ...Monday...

...

**GREG.** —Does anyone else hear?

...

<u>**LB (EXCEPT JACOB).** *whistling ...??? /*</u>

**HANNAH.** It can't be?

**TUTTLE.** Is someone like—

...

<u>**LB (EXCEPT JACOB).** *?...happy...?*</u>

...

      **JACOB.** *; )* Hey Everyone *; )*

<u>**GREG, MITRA, TUTTLE.** *Jacob???*</u>

    <u>**HANNAH.** What the fuck?</u>

        <u>**NICOLE.** shit /</u>

    **JACOB.** Quick "Announcement."—Mitra, love the chimichurri /

**MITRA.** Thanks...

**JACOB.** Natalie—

**GREG.** *(Cough.)* Nicole

**NICOLE.** ...yeah?/?

**JACOB.** Just wanted to let you know you're off the hook on Mondays – since Tal's coming back – from Paris

**NICOLE.**

oh...uh...okay?/

<u>**GREG & TUTTLE.** *David/...*</u>

**HANNAH.** *pretzels/...*

**JACOB.** *(To* **GREG, TUTTLE, HANNAH.***)* —Don't (talk about) *(To* **NICOLE.***)* Of course, we'll let you know if we're ever looking for "a sub." But you know, *"Cheeses."* Everyone loves *"Cheeses."* Even Greg – resident "vegan"—You understand

**NICOLE.**

of course. "Got it." / Thanks...

**JACOB.** Well that was Painless! / All right, BREAK

**MITRA.** —Wait —Actually

—Hey Guys...?!

**HANNAH.** fuck /

<u>**JACOB.** *whhAAAA(t?!)*        **NICOLE.** What are you doing?</u>

**MITRA.** I thought I mentioned it— I'm doing Whole 30!

<u>**HANNAH.** fuck /</u>

<u>**TUTTLE.** what! /</u>

<u>**JACOB.** *Whole?* /</u>

**MITRA.** **30.** No sugar. No grains. No dairy. No beans. No MSG. No alcohol. No fun. Basically: organic meats and veggies. And I'm a vegetarian so that means:

<u>**MITRA & TUTTLE.** VEGGIES!!!</u>

**JACOB.** *I KNOW WHAT WHOLE 30 IS*

**MITRA.** Tuttle inspired me [**TUTTLE.** Awh, **JACOB.** Tuttle.] "Sugar is poison, dairy is poison" [**TUTTLE.** – in pink – ]

—Nicole, would you mind taking over for me?

**JACOB.** That's not / how it—

**NICOLE.** *Seriously?* —/ you don't

**MITRA.** You'd be doing me a *Huge* favor

**NICOLE.**

   thank you /

**MITRA.** Don't mention it

     **JACOB.** Mitra, Can I speak with you?

**MITRA.** sure…

           …

     **JACOB.** Over here. To the side. An aside maybe?

**MITRA.** Okay…

      —What's up?

     **JACOB.** Your "Fiesta Corn Salad" has *Cotija*

**MITRA.** …/?

**JACOB.** Last week you said Hannah's "Spanakopita" was "great"

**MITRA.** I had a change of heart

**JACOB.** …/

**MITRA.** I watched a *Documentary* /

**JACOB.** Which. One

**MITRA.** —/

**JACOB.** —Forks over Knives?Cowspiracy?*Fed Up?!*

**MITRA.** It was French…/

**JACOB.** I'm gonna let you in on a "little secret": Everything's bad
   for you!!!

**MITRA.** I don't think I like you. How you…treat…people

**JACOB.** That's the thing – about Lunch Bunch – You don't have to

—Where are you going? Don't— Don't walk away from me! —We'll go dairy free?!

**MITRA**. Bye Jacob

**JACOB.** FUCK!

FUCK

FUCK ME

LSDKFJLDSKJFSLKDFJLWEIJRSLDKF/MKDJFOIWEJ
FSDLKJFALSKDJFLWIEJFLSKJFLKSDJFSOIEJRSDLK
MVLSIEJFSLKDNVKXJRIWEJFSLKDJFLSKDJFSKDJA
KDJFLKSLSKDJFIERUEWLIJSKVMEXJDIJASJLFAKSJ
DLFKJSDLFKJSLDKJFALKSDJFLKAJSDFLKF!!!!

**TUTTLE, HANNAH, GREG, MITRA, NICOLE**. I'M A WRENCH

I'M A WRENCH

I'M A WRENCH

FUCKING UP THE MACHINE AHHHHHHHHHH /

...

...

...

---

**DAVID**. I came to in what appeared to be a savannah. With nothing save my court blazer, a Hydro Flask of cold brew, and a half-eaten bag of        *...pretzels*

A seemingly minor misinterpretation of what constitutes "a side dish," and here I am, crawling through some (?)Late Stone Age(?) *(?)era(?)*

In desperation, I reached for my phone – news of my expulsion had arrived via group text – but its screen, like my surroundings, had faded to black

I was: completely alone and...utterly defenseless...

In the days – *(?)weeks(?)* – that followed I wandered the savannah in search of sustenance, shelter, Some Sign of My Species. I tailed an antelope for several hours who eventually led me to the local watering hole – where I was able to refill my Hydro Flask. I made crude tools by banging various rocks together, which I then used to procure roots and tubers —Without the ability to cook and thereby soften these foraged fares, I was forced to spend roughly Five Hours A Day *chewing*. In the evenings, I removed my increasingly ragged court blazer and massaged my weary jaw —I missed my dog, but humans wouldn't domesticate animals for another few thousand years – And so, I retired, with the sun, in the branches of low hanging trees, my loneliness enveloping me in lieu of a blanket —I *"Survived,"* sure – Narrowly dodging death by cave lions, some larger primates, starvation, drought, disease, the occasional ill-chosen nut or berry – *And yet,* without the company of my kind, my survival lacked *Meaning* I stopped taking care of my body and prepared myself to pass, ascending a nearby promontory in search of a final resting place

...

However,

It was on this mount that I first saw *Smoke* – A lone column rising *(?)north(?)* and *(?)east(?). Wherein,* a forgotten sense stirred me:

*"Could it be...!?!?"*

*"? fire ?"*

"Harnessed by my fellow early-modern humans ?!"

I tasted: *hope*

And set out: Again

...

Beneath the smoke, I spied a band of seven roasting the remains of some...*less fortunate*...animal. I approached them – cautiously – then crouched behind a bush so that I might observe them from a discreet distance. When finally, I worked up the courage to reveal myself, they ceased their occupation straightaway —Of course, I was used to this sort of thing. The twenty-first century had inured me to rejection. And so, I *Waited.* Whilst they *"Conferred,"* over the inevitable unfolding of my fate and what smelled like *(?)slightly sweet(?),* Perfectly Smoked, *Flesh* —Despite my devotion to a predominantly plant-based diet for the bulk of my consciousness, I *Salivated* for: *(???)BBQ(???)* and ***Acceptance**** Until*, one of them, who appeared to be some sort of leader or *(?)spokesperson(?)* stepped forward and – *in a gesture that required no translation and a language not unlike modern day French –* offered me *A Bite* of some, Prehistoric, *(French accent.) Sandwich:*

      —"T'en veux?"

    *(French accent.)* —"*Antilope?*"

| | |
|---|---|
| I became: | one of them |
| And Subsequently: | *Survived* |

**TAL.**   —David?

**DAVID.**              —I'm on the fourth floor now

                —(I got a—) motion to file

                —Later

                ...

                ...

                ...

**TAL**. Hey guys!!!

**LB**. !?TAL!?

You're back!          **TAL**. I'm back!

**TAL**. —Who wants :

**TAL, NICOLE, GREG, HANNAH**.      **TUTTLE & MITRA**.
Cheeses???                    cheeses...

**TAL**. Lots and lots of :

**TAL, NICOLE, GREG, HANNAH**       **TUTTLE & MITRA**
*Cheeses!!!*                   cheeses : (

**TAL & NICOLE**. Brie!/

**TAL & GREG**. Camembert!/

**TAL & HANNAH**. Comté!/

**TAL, MITRA, TUTTLE**. Morbier?!/

**TAL, NICOLE, GREG, HANNAH, TUTTLE, MITRA**.
Tome des / (Bauges) :

**TAL**. *(French accent.) Ahn Ahn Ahn !*      *Not Yet ; )*

**TAL, NICOLE, GREG, HANNAH**.      **TUTTLE & MITRA**.
*—BAGUETTES?!?!*          ; ( baguettes ; (

**JACOB**. I think I'm gonna be sick

**GREG**. It'll / (pass)

**JACOB**. No, really, sick

—Are there peppers in this???

**MITRA**. shit

OhMyGod

Shit! Jacob I'm so—

...

It was a—

...

shit

...

**TAL.**  Is he—

**GREG.**  vomiting. Yeah

**TUTTLE.**  In the coat ???

**GREG.**  Yep

...

.../

*

*(The* **LUNCH BUNCH** *now includes* **NICOLE, JACOB, HANNAH, GREG,** *and* **TAL.***)*

**LB.**  THURSDAY

**GREG.**  BLACK BEANS, BROWN RICE, STEAMED BOK CHOY, SPICED TOFU

...

...

**TUTTLE.**  *(On the phone.)* Hi yes this is—

—From

Uh huh, Uh huh, Uh huh

...

I spoke with ACS and they're gonna—

They're gonna (move the kids)          yeah

**TUTTLE.**  —Do you have anyone else who could (take them)

—We're gonna file another (motion), I just

—We need a (plan)

...

I'm sorry

Okay, I'll—

okay

...

**GREG.**  Brought you your Lunch Bunch

—And some cheeses – if you're...up to it

—Honey ginger tofu – For digestion

**JACOB.**

—What's this?

**GREG.**

napkin

**JACOB.**

—I can't read your writing

...

**GREG.**  "Desiring lasts a long time. Demands and requests go on to infinity. Fulfillment is short and is meted out sparingly. Even the final satisfaction itself, in the end, is only superficial. The wish fulfillment at once making way for a new one"

It seemed relevant—to your: "struggle"

**JACOB.** You mean *"Natalie"*

**GREG.**

Is it possible *Nicole* is a symptom. Not *"The Problem"*

**JACOB.**

Is this from "your book?"

**GREG.** *It's—* Schopenhauer /

**JACOB.** I only read women and people of color

**GREG.** It was quoted – In an essay. By Zadie Smith

**JACOB.**

I'm bored of this. I'm bored of you

**GREG.** *Want and boredom the twin poles of human life*

**JACOB.** *one*

*week*

**GREG.** I think the fulfillment of your desire would lead to despair – Or more desires

Probably both

**JACOB.** Leave me

...

...

**GREG.** What are you listening to?

**JACOB.** Lana Del Rey

**GREG.**

I have to go to court

Otherwise I'd stay. And DJ

...

>           **MITRA.**  Hey Jacob. I just wanted to apologize –
>           again – for last week

>                                ...

>                                ...

**MITRA.**  —Is he...?asleep?/

**HANNAH.**  Don't (touch him)

**MITRA.**  —Can you *?sleep?* ?standing up? —With your eyes
*?open?*

**HANNAH.**  He does this – Sometimes

It's like meditating

**MITRA.**

**HANNAH.**  But more depressing

**MITRA.**

—Can he *?hear us?*

**HANNAH.**  hard to say

**MITRA.**

I feel like we should ?do something?/

**HANNAH.**  Sometimes it's best...Not to

>                                ...

>           **MITRA.**  —Gotta get back to /

**HANNAH & MITRA.**  <u>Intake /</u>

>      **MITRA.**  yeah

**HANNAH.** congrats        —I heard

>      **MITRA.**

thanks...

Later

...

...

...

**TUTTLE**.  Oh wow. He's doing it again

—Is it me or are things falling apart slash going
to shit more than usual around here?

...

**HANNAH**.  Haven't noticed

...

**TUTTLE**.  This person I was sleeping with, Well once –
A few times actually – in the same night —It was
"Condensed." We haven't talked since, but I stalk them
online – Occasionally. As one (does)— What was I— Oh!
They're doing this work – *"IMPACT-ivism."* About
how people *want* to do "good," *try* to do "good," have
these "good" *intentions*, but then fail to follow up and
or measure the results of their "Actions." It's about how
sometimes(?) instead of our "Good" "Deeds" making
matters *Better*, they're actually making matters worse...
—Or, alternatively, expending a lot of energy and
resources for very little result... Basically they're trying
to combat(?) or confront(?) the issue of: Doing "Good"
to Feel "Good" – about ourselves – instead of to impact
change

I don't feel good —Is that how you know you're making
an impact? The complete absence of that warm fuzzy
feeling?

**HANNAH**.

I don't have the emotional energy to have this
conversation with you

**TUTTLE.**

**HANNAH.**  —sorry

**TUTTLE.**  No—

I respect that. I like that you have:        *Boundaries*

**HANNAH.**

I have to go deal with this emergency removal

**TUTTLE.**  shit

**HANNAH.**  yeah

**TUTTLE.**  —Oh, hey —Have you seen Mitra? I made coconut almond butter bites (—They're) "Whole 30 Friendly"

**HANNAH.**  (She's on—) intake. You just missed her

**TUTTLE.**  OU! I almost forgot/!

**HANNAH.**  She asked Judge White for a 1028 [**TUTTLE.** *She didn't!*] Who knows, we might have a new Kween

**TUTTLE.**

You'll always be our Kween

—with a K at least—

**HANNAH.**  ; )

I'm out

**TUTTLE.**  —client meeting. *Eaughk!* I'll go with you

...

...

...

(**TAL** *remembers "...Paris !"*)

.../

**NICOLE.**  Hey

—Where is everyone?

**TAL.**  Court? Client meetings? Coat closet?

—It's / ?Natalie?

**NICOLE.**  Nicole /

**TAL.**  right

**NICOLE.**  "Training Team One"

**TAL.**

—What's up?

**NICOLE.**  I was keeping an eye on some of your cases – Hannah was supervising – She said I should brief you

**TAL.**  Anything / (happen?)

**NICOLE.**  Not really. Couple missed programs here. Couple missed court appearances there. None of the ACS attorneys returning my emails —FIVE CLIENTS on my first intake /

**TAL.**  yii/iiikes

**NICOLE.**  yeaaah but that doesn't involve *You* —Oh! And! That really sweet guy with the —!

**TAL.**  Ricky?

**NICOLE.**  *Yes! Ricky!* He violated his order of protection but we're hoping the judge doesn't find o/ut

**TAL.**  Oh god. What did he / (do?)

**NICOLE.**  NOTHING. So dumb. What a mess. We'll fix it — I feel like there was something good.............................

.................................................................................

no... can't remember —Oh No WAIT! We got unsupervised visits for Mr. Ramírez!! /

**TAL**.  REALLY/?

**NICOLE**.  YEAH/!

**TAL**.  THAT'S GREAT/!

**NICOLE**.  ISN'T IT/!?

**TAL**.  —How did you/???

**NICOLE**.  ACS was worried we'd file a 1028 /

**TAL**.  Wait, what, (Please tell me—) you did/n't—?

**NICOLE**.  HAHAHA-NO ohmygod-*SCARY!* BuuuuuuT I might have "Suggested It" *forcefully ?* —Hannah's idea. Not a "Threat," But also, not *Not-A-Threat* – if you / (know what I)

**TAL**.  —that worked?!

**NICOLE**.  ?!Apparently!?

**TAL**.

He must be really happy

**NICOLE**.  —said he's been going to "The Gym" /

**TAL**.  the / gym?

**NICOLE**.  Next Up: Overnight Visits!

…

**TAL**.  Thanks for keeping an eye on my cases

**NICOLE**.

you're welcome

**TAL**.  You're good

—at this—

**NICOLE**.  —Really? I mean— Thanks. Thank You. "Confidence"

…

**TAL.**  —Was there something else you wanted to...?

...

**NICOLE.**  the recipe

**TAL.**  ?/?

**NICOLE.**  – for your BBQ jackfruit / sandwich –

**TAL.**  wh/at?

**NICOLE.**  BBQ jackfruit sandwich

**TAL.**  ...?

**NICOLE.**  Will you send it to me? —I mean as long as it's not

a family "recipe" / or ?

**TAL.**  I think it was the first thing that popped up when I
googled it

**NICOLE.**  I keep finding my Lunch Bunch, barely eaten, in the trash

And last week – I made smashed chickpea and avocado salad sandwiches

**TAL.**  that sounds good/?

**NICOLE.**  I THOUGHT SO TOO!!

But,

I found one

—I think it was:

Jacob's—

And it wasn't missing a bite

Not one

bite

**TAL.**  I'll send it to you

.../

*

**NICOLE, HANNAH, GREG, TAL.** <u>MONDAY</u>

**NICOLE.**   —

Wait

**NICOLE, HANNAH, GREG, TAL.**   —<u>Where's</u>

**NICOLE, HANNAH, GREG, TAL.**   ...

...

**MITRA.**  Hey. Your French Thing —It's gone?

**HANNAH.**  Oh yeah, it drained – Spontaneously

—Hot compress four times a day for weeks on end, and then, one morning, you wake up and BOOM. Lotta goo

**MITRA.**  That's /...

**TUTTLE.**  awful /

**HANNAH.**  The body does some weird shit when you're not looking

**TUTTLE.**

*(To "The French Thing.")* We'll miss you

<u>**HANNAH & MITRA.**</u>

<u>???</u>

...

**HANNAH.**  —What are you eating? —Is that *?cheese?*

**TUTTLE.**  Yeahhh. I found some Roquefort in the back of my fridge. I can't tell if the smell means it's really bad or really good —I finished Whole 30. Turns out I'm not allergic...To anything

<u>**MITRA.** sorry</u>              <u>**HANNAH.** congrats</u>

**TUTTLE.**

I changed the background – on my phone

**MITRA.**  What's it / (say?)

...

...

...

**MITRA.**  oh wow

...

**HANNAH.**  That's deep

...

       **TAL.**  Hey, what'd y'all do this weekend?

     —Oh snap it drained

**HANNAH, MITRA, TUTTLE.**  – Spontaneously –

**TAL.**

(*To* **TUTTLE.**) —Is that /

**TUTTLE.**  Cheese —I'm not allergic – " Yay "

**TAL.**  (*To* **MITRA.**) Not to be— But are you—.../*?glowing?*

**MITRA.**  I started training for a half marathon this weekend

**TAL.**  Woah, what are you like – *?well-adjusted?*

**MITRA.**  Ha, no, I wish. I got wasted by myself the Monday before I started Whole 30. My ex – who was really into serial cheating on me and now has some sort of obscure cancer, sent me a mass email – a race for the cure type thing – and for some reason I signed up to run thirteen miles and raise money for him

**TAL.**

That's dark /

**MITRA**.  Yeah —You?

**TAL**.  Netflix. Lots and lots of Netflix. Lil HBO. Amazon
Prime. I really want Hulu…

**TUTTLE**.  I think Nicole has Hulu

**TAL**.  Ouuuu. I'll ask ; )

   …What else…

   —I finished all of my *Cheeses* /

**TUTTLE & MITRA**.  Awh

**TAL**.  Then edited and posted the rest of the pics—from
my trip

| **TUTTLE & MITRA**. | **HANNAH**. |
|---|---|
| I liked them | I don't do "social media" |

**TAL**.

   *blushing*

   —guess I'll get back on "the wagon" this week

                              …

**TAL**.  —Hey Greg

   **GREG**.  Hey

**TAL**.  What'd you do this weekend?

**GREG**.  Some pre-seeding for my roof garden Saturday.
Volunteering Sunday

**TAL**.  What do you—/?

**GREG**.  —Basil, mint, habaneros —Tax prep for low income
families and individuals

**TAL**. shit

**GREG**.  I'm gonna make hot sauce I think

**TAL.** —*Spicy Tofu?!*

**GREG.** ...

maybe

    **NICOLE.** Hey. Has anyone seen—

...

**NICOLE, HANNAH, GREG, TAL, TUTTLE, MITRA.**

...Jacob...

    **JACOB.** ...

...

**TAL.** Oh man, he looks...*Awful*

**GREG.** One of his clients was arrested Friday. Think he spent most of the weekend dealing with that—

**TAL.** Geezus

—You want me to/?

**GREG.** I got this

**TAL.**

Backup – If ya need it

...

...

**GREG.** Hey buddy. How's it going?

**JACOB.**

**GREG.** Heard you had a rough weekend

**JACOB.**

**GREG.**

You look a little—

**JACOB.**

**GREG.**  —I made coffee

**JACOB.**

**GREG.**

I can grab some

—if you

**JACOB.**

**GREG.**  Buddy?

**JACOB.**  I figured it out

**GREG.**  ?/?

**JACOB.**  *The Perfect Week*

**GREG.**

I thought we / (talked about all this)

**JACOB.**  MONDAY: Southwestern Quinoa Bowl with honey lime dressing

TUESDAY: Vegan Sancocho and chocolate chia pudding

WEDNESDAY: Cucumber Avocado Tea Sandwiches with dill and mint

THURSDAY: I'm actually starting to look forward to your / Brown Rice Black Beans Seasonal Steamed Veggie plus Spiced Tofu

**GREG.**  brown rice black beans seasonal steamed veggie plus spiced tofu

—I don't believe you /

**JACOB.**  It's true. FRIDAY:

*Pumpkin Seed Pesto Pizza with*
*Cauliflower Crust*

**GREG**.  Jacob… That's… quite a week /

**JACOB**.   !BUT!, it's not over, Because Then There's: "The Weekend"—Which I'll begin with: SUSHI – from my favorite take-out spot. Macrobiotic Crunchy Shallot Roll with Flaxseed Rice side Seaweed Salad. SATURDAY: I'll take my dog /

**GREG**.  You have a / dog?

**JACOB**.  No. For a walk. I'll do some work, no way around that, but I'll do it at a café as I nibble on a Raspberry Sprouted Spelt Scone, whilst making eyes at the man sitting at the table across from me, *who* – is also working – and *who* looks like, he just might, know how to preserve a lemon – without googling. I'll do this instead of working from home – in my onesie – as I often slash always do /

**GREG**.  I have a one/sie

**JACOB**.  We all do

WHICH BRINGS ME TO: SUNDAY, when I'll go to Trader Joe's! —Let me stop you, I know what you're thinking, "Jacob, you're crazy! TRADER JOE'S?! SUNDAY?! DO YOU HAVE A DEATH WISH?!," But see, that's where you're wrong! Because *this time* there won't be a line, Because *This Time* is not any time. *This Time* is *Jacob's Perfect Week.* Everyone's "asleep," or at ""Smorgasburg."" I'll wander the aisles, reflecting on myself, the state of the world, my relation to slash position in it, the past week. Trader Joe's, Grocery shopping: Something akin to mass? service? synagogue? spin? I'll stumble across a new spice – something like ?Dukkah? – which I'll buy, and then both eagerly(?) and absently(?) scroll through new recipes, on my phone, the whole way home. Once I'm back, I'll do a little prep – for Tuesday. Perhaps soak some chickpeas – or cashews, if I'm planning on making a cream. As I crawl into bed, my phone rings.

**JACOB.** A coworker(?) friend(?) you(?) maybe, calling. Did I know – Judge White's retiring(!) and someone who actually has a heart and a background in family court is replacing him! Effective immediately?!?! Also:

"thanks"

"Thank you"

I'm not sure for what. But for something

good(?)

I did

maybe

I'm turning into Tuttle. I keep having these night terrors...

**GREG.**

**JACOB.** —Is it Friday? —What day is it? I forget—

**GREG.** ?/?

**JACOB.** —It feels like it's / (been)

**GREG.** Monday

**JACOB.**

...Natalie...

**GREG.**

Nicole

(**JACOB** *crawls under his "desk."*)

**GREG.** What—? Where are you / (going)—?

**JACOB.**

I'm an ostrich

          ...

          ...

    **NICOLE**.  Hey. Have you seen

     ...?

     Jacob?

**GREG**.  Uhm...

  ...

**NICOLE**.  I have his lunch

**GREG**.  ...

**NICOLE**.  – bunch –

He didn't respond to the group text. I'm not sure where
he wants it

**GREG**.  You can leave it

– here –

I'll make sure he gets it

**NICOLE**.  Thanks

—Yours is in the fridge

**GREG**.  looking forward

**NICOLE**.

—Do you want me to / (grab it?)

**GREG**.  I'll get it. Just gonna finish up a few emails first

     ...

**NICOLE**.  Can I—Uh—

**GREG**.  ?/?

**NICOLE.**  Will you make sure he tries it? —Sorry / You don't (have to—)

**GREG.** You got it

**NICOLE.**

    thanks

               ...

               ...

               ...

**JACOB.**  —Is she gone?

               ...

               ...

**GREG.**  Yeah, she's eating at her desk

**JACOB.**

    I'm afraid to open it

**GREG.**

    What is it?

**JACOB.**

    Some sort of meatless...sandwich?

    smells like BBQ

    side salad

**GREG.**

    Are you gonna / (try it)

(**JACOB** *takes a bite. Chews...*)

**GREG.**  How is it?/

**JACOB.**  Good

**GREG.**

Are you / (crying?)

**JACOB.**  It's really—

(*To* **NICOLE.**) Thank you

The sandwich. It's really—

thanks

Thank you

(**NICOLE** *and* **JACOB** *chew.*)

(*Blackout.*)

**End of Play**

www.ingramcontent.com/pod-product-compliance
Lightning Source LLC
Chambersburg PA
CBHW070416120726

47909CB00005B/1673